KUNG FU ROAD TRIP

adapted by Tina Gallo

Ready-to-Read

Simon Spotlight

New York   London   Toronto   Sydney   New Delhi

SIMON SPOTLIGHT
An imprint of Simon & Schuster Children's Publishing Division
1230 Avenue of the Americas, New York, New York 10020
Kung Fu Panda Legends of Awesomeness
© 2014 Viacom International Inc.
NICKELODEON and all related logos are trademarks of
Viacom International Inc. Based on the feature film "Kung Fu Panda" © 2008 DreamWorks
Animation L.L.C. All Rights Reserved.
SIMON SPOTLIGHT, READY-TO-READ, and colophon are registered trademarks of Simon & Schuster, Inc.
For information about special discounts for bulk purchases, please contact Simon & Schuster Special Sales at
1-866-506-1949 or business@simonandschuster.com.
Manufactured in the United States of America 0514 LAK
First Edition
2 4 6 8 10 9 7 5 3 1
ISBN 978-1-4814-0488-4 (pbk)
ISBN 978-1-4814-0489-1 (hc)
ISBN 978-1-4814-0490-7 (eBook)

"We are taking a vacation,"
Shifu announced.

Po and the Furious Five gasped. They weren't getting along. "You want us to spend more time with each other?" Monkey asked.

"Yes," Shifu said firmly. "We are going to the Secret Museum of Kung Fu."

Shifu told Po and the Furious Five about the museum. "Centuries ago, the masters built it to keep China's most powerful weapons safe."

"There is only one key to the museum, and one map to reveal its location," Shifu said. "And I bought them both."

"It's important that no one sees a group of kung fu masters traveling to the museum," said Shifu. "We don't want to give away its location." "We can go in disguise in my dad's noodle mobile," Po offered.

"Excellent," Shifu said. "It will give me a chance to wear my false beard."

The next day, the group squeezed into the noodle mobile.

"Dibs on the back seat!" shouted Crane.

"I'm already in the back seat," Monkey said.

"But you didn't call dibs," Crane pointed out.

"I'm sitting here. That's automatic dibs," Monkey said.

"There's no automatic dibs," Crane retorted.

"Don't make me come back there!" Shifu yelled.

Po decided to do a magic trick. He wanted to amaze the Furious Five by escaping out of handcuffs. "One, two, three, behold!" he said grandly, but he was still handcuffed.

"Great trick, Po," Mantis said.
He sounded bored.

The group had no idea that they were being followed by some wolves. "Once we have the map to the Secret Museum, the Phantom Crystal will be ours," their leader said.

The wolves stopped the noodle
mobile.
Their leader grabbed the map.
He also grabbed the key, but Shifu
didn't know it.

Once they had gotten away,
the wolves opened Shifu's map.
It was blank!
"We will have to follow them to the
museum," their leader said.

Meanwhile, Po and the Furious Five were back on the road.
They were still arguing!
Shifu turned around to stop them.
There was no one watching where the noodle mobile was headed.
Soon, they were zooming down a steep hill.

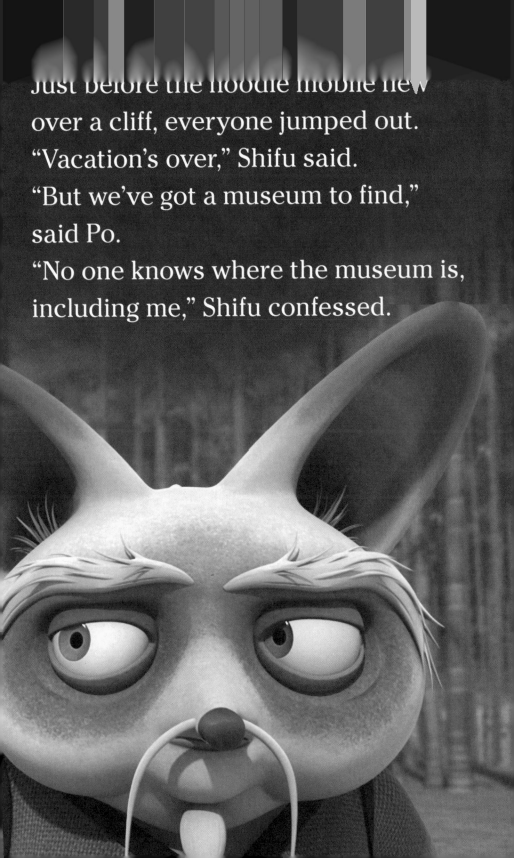

Just before the noodle mobile flew over a cliff, everyone jumped out.
"Vacation's over," Shifu said.
"But we've got a museum to find," said Po.
"No one knows where the museum is, including me," Shifu confessed.

"But you had a map," Po said.

"The map was blank," Shifu replied.
"I thought the journey would help
us bond. Since you don't want to
be a team, you're all on your own."
Shifu walked away.

Everyone else walked off too.

"Some vacation," Po said.

A few minutes later, Shifu stumbled across a stone with a symbol carved into it.

Shifu looked up.
"I found the Secret Museum!"
he cried.
He reached into his pocket
for the key.
"Looking for this?" someone snarled.
It was the wolf leader.
He was holding the key!

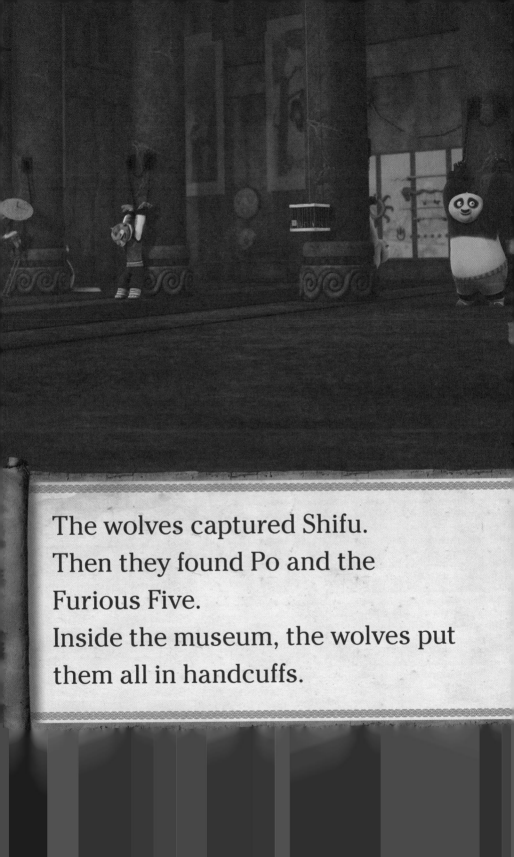

The wolves captured Shifu.
Then they found Po and the
Furious Five.
Inside the museum, the wolves put
them all in handcuffs.

The wolf leader grabbed the Phantom Crystal.
"With the Phantom Crystal, no walls can stop me!" he cried. "All the riches of the world will be mine!"

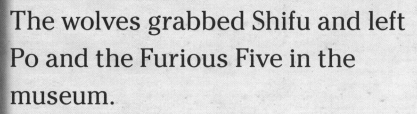

The wolves grabbed Shifu and left
Po and the Furious Five in the
museum.
There was no way out.
"Worst vacation ever," said Tigress.

Po had a familiar question for the group.

"Who wants to see a magic trick?" he asked.

"No one!" shouted Viper.

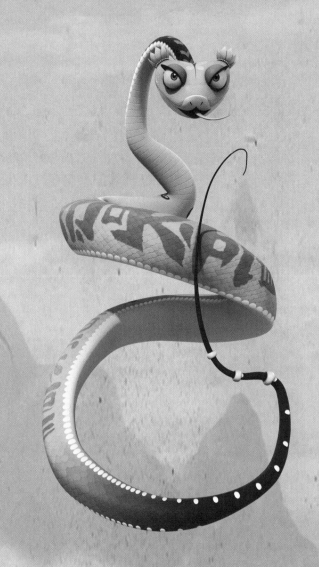

"Behold!" Po announced.
He was out of the handcuffs!
He helped the others get free.
"We can split up again if you want,"
Po said. "Or we could work as a
team to save Shifu."
They all agreed to work together.

Po found the wolf leader.
He was admiring the Phantom
Crystal.
"This thing is amazing!" he said.
"It does look pretty cool," Po
agreed.

The wolf leader was shocked to see
Po and the Furious Five.
"Destroy them!" he shouted to the
other wolves.
Everyone began fighting.

The wolf leader thought he had won
the battle with Po.
"Any last words?" he asked.
"Yes," Po answered. "Behold!"
Po had the Phantom Crystal!
"Best trick ever," Po said.

Po, Shifu, and the Furious Five
defeated the wolves.
"Working together, there's nothing
we can't do," Shifu said.
"Absolutely," Po said. "All in all,
this was a pretty good trip."
Everyone agreed.

"And we should never do it again,"
Po added.

Everyone agreed with this too.

"Now you sound like a team!" Shifu
said proudly.